I call my Grandma

and everyone can see
that I love spending time with her
and she loves being with me.

**For all the wonderful grandmothers I know,
especially Granny Deane and
Grandmasaurus Jewell.**

Text and Illustrations copyright © 2009 by Ashley Wolff

Tricycle Press
an imprint of Ten Speed Press
PO Box 7123
Berkeley, California 94707
www.tricyclepress.com

Design by Susan Van Horn
Typeset in Cheltenham
The illustrations in this book were created using gouache and collage.

Library of Congress Cataloging-in-Publication Data

Wolff, Ashley.
I call my grandma Nana / by Ashley Wolff.
p. cm.
Summary: Students respond, in rhyming text, to their teacher's question
about what each calls his or her grandmother, offering examples of things
they like to do together.
ISBN-13: 978-1-58246-251-6 (hardcover)
ISBN-10: 1-58246-251-8 (hardcover)
[1. Stories in rhyme. 2. Grandmothers–Fiction. 3. Names,
Personal–Fiction.] I. Title.
PZ8.3.W843Iac 2009
[E]–dc22
2008042183

First Tricycle Press printing, 2009
Printed in Singapore

1 2 3 4 5 6 — 13 12 11 10 09

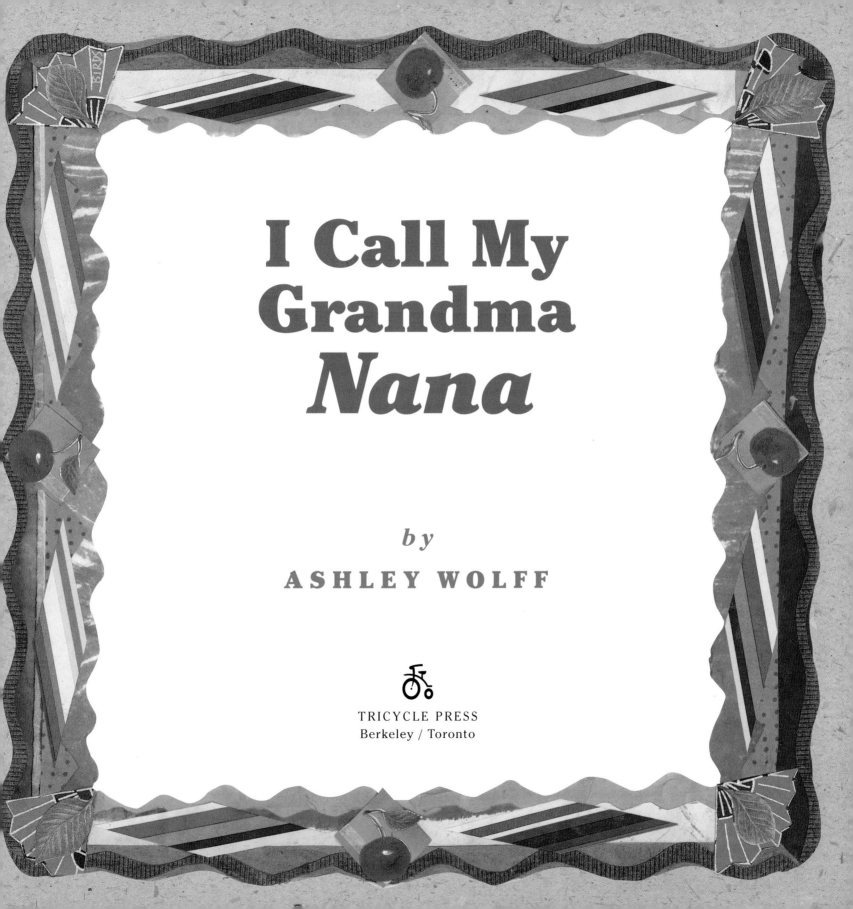

I Call My Grandma *Nana*

by

ASHLEY WOLFF

TRICYCLE PRESS
Berkeley / Toronto

"My grandmother from China
is visiting today.
Class, please welcome **Nai-Nai**,"
said Miss Alexandra May.

"Our Grandmas all have stories—
no two are just the same.
They have so much to teach us
and deserve their special names.

Will you please tell Nai-Nai
about these pictures that you drew
of you and all your grandmas
and what you love to do?"

My Nonna
and me in
her garden.
Carlo

My Yaya lets
me lick the
bowl. Ben

Rosie said, "Let me go first!
In this picture that I drew,
I'm paddling with my **Grammy**
in our brand-new, red canoe."

Grammy

Me

I went in a boat
with my Grammy.

Rosie

"My **Oba-Chan** folds paper.
She made a purple crane.
Now I'm going to teach her
how to fly a plane!"

"**Abuelita** is my Grandma.
She's teaching me to sew.
The doll we're making
    looks like me—
blue dress, black braid,
    white bow!"

"My **Granny** has a telescope.
We love to look at stars.
I've seen the Little Dipper
and the bright, red planet Mars."

"My **Lola** has a million blocks
and wooden tracks and cranes.
We build a town—and all around
I get to drive my trains."

"My **Mamie** likes the hummingbirds.
I always look for jays.
I carry her binoculars
on our bird-watching days."

"My **Bubbe** says next summer,
she hopes that I will teach
her how to ride a boogie board
when we're at the beach."

"**Naani** is my real grandma,
but she lives so far away.
So Ruth is **Next-Door-Nana**
when I need a hug today!"

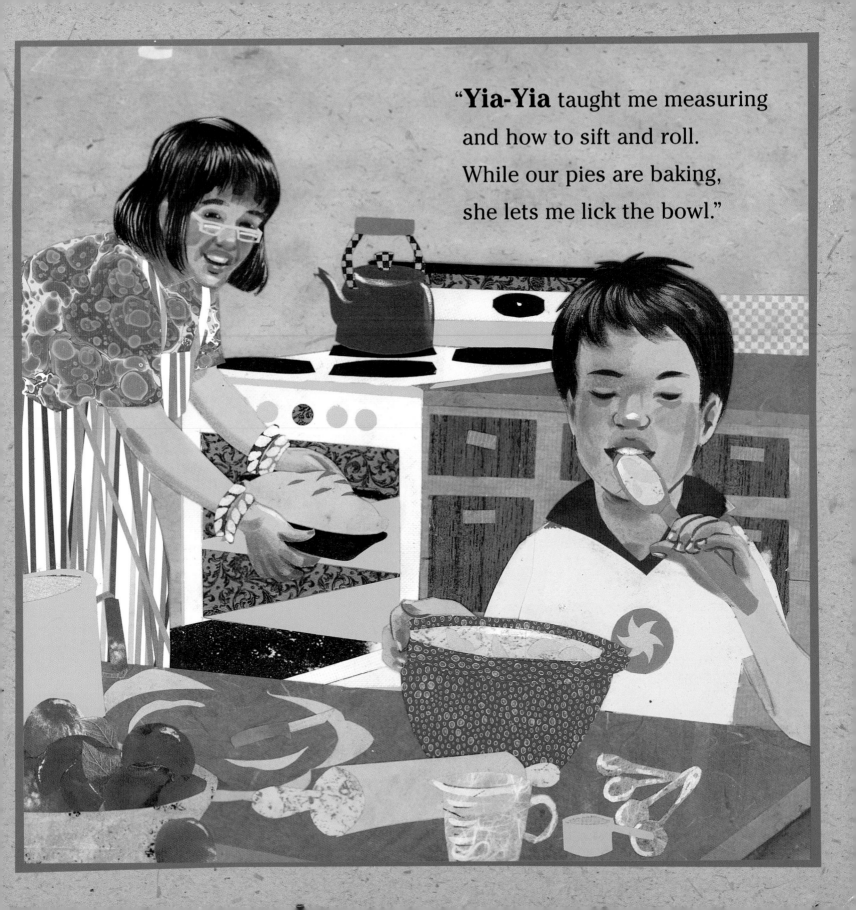

"**Yia-Yia** taught me measuring
and how to sift and roll.
While our pies are baking,
she lets me lick the bowl."

"My **Nonna** grows tomatoes
and corn and beans and plums.
She says that I've inherited
both of her green thumbs!"

"I spent a week with **Oma** while Mommy was away. We ate pepperoni pizza for our breakfast everyday!"

"My **MeMaw** is a pilot.
Her job is in the air.
But on the ground, we drive around
with breezes in our hair."

"I have four **grandmothers**!
You wouldn't want to hear
how they sang me 'Happy Birthday'
on that noisy day last year!"

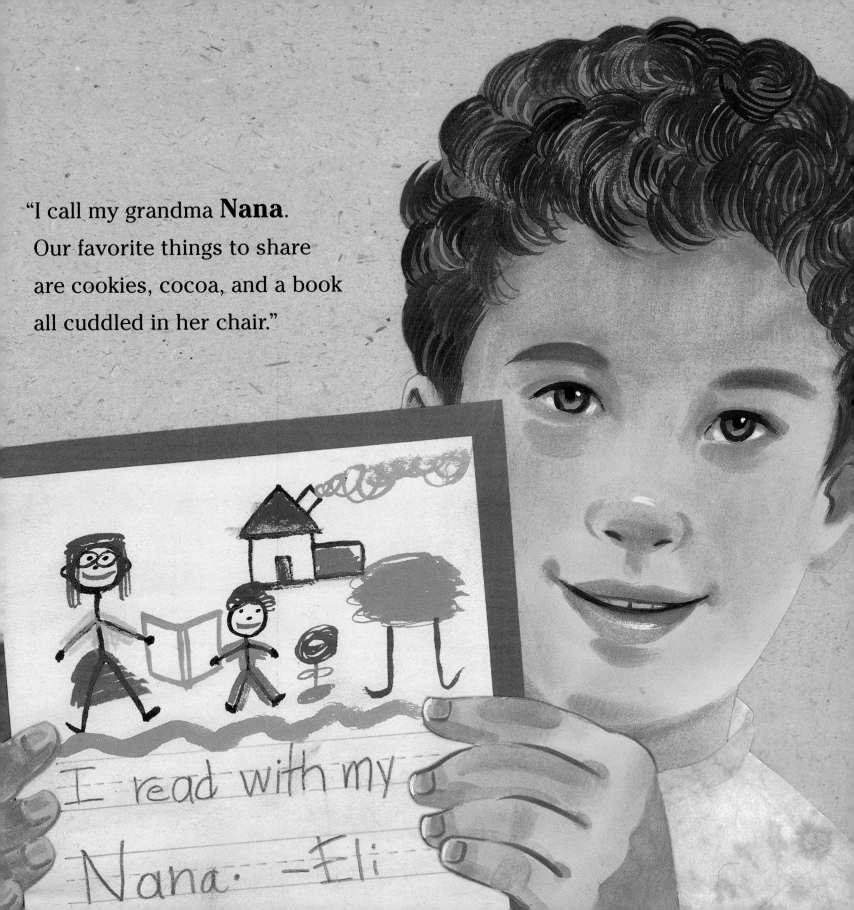

"I call my grandma **Nana**.
Our favorite things to share
are cookies, cocoa, and a book
all cuddled in her chair."

I read with my
Nana. —Eli

"Thank you, Eli," said Miss May,
"And thank you everyone
for telling us your grandma's name,
and what you do for fun.

You are their precious young ones,
and I can guarantee
that they'll love you just as dearly...

when you're all grown up, like me!"